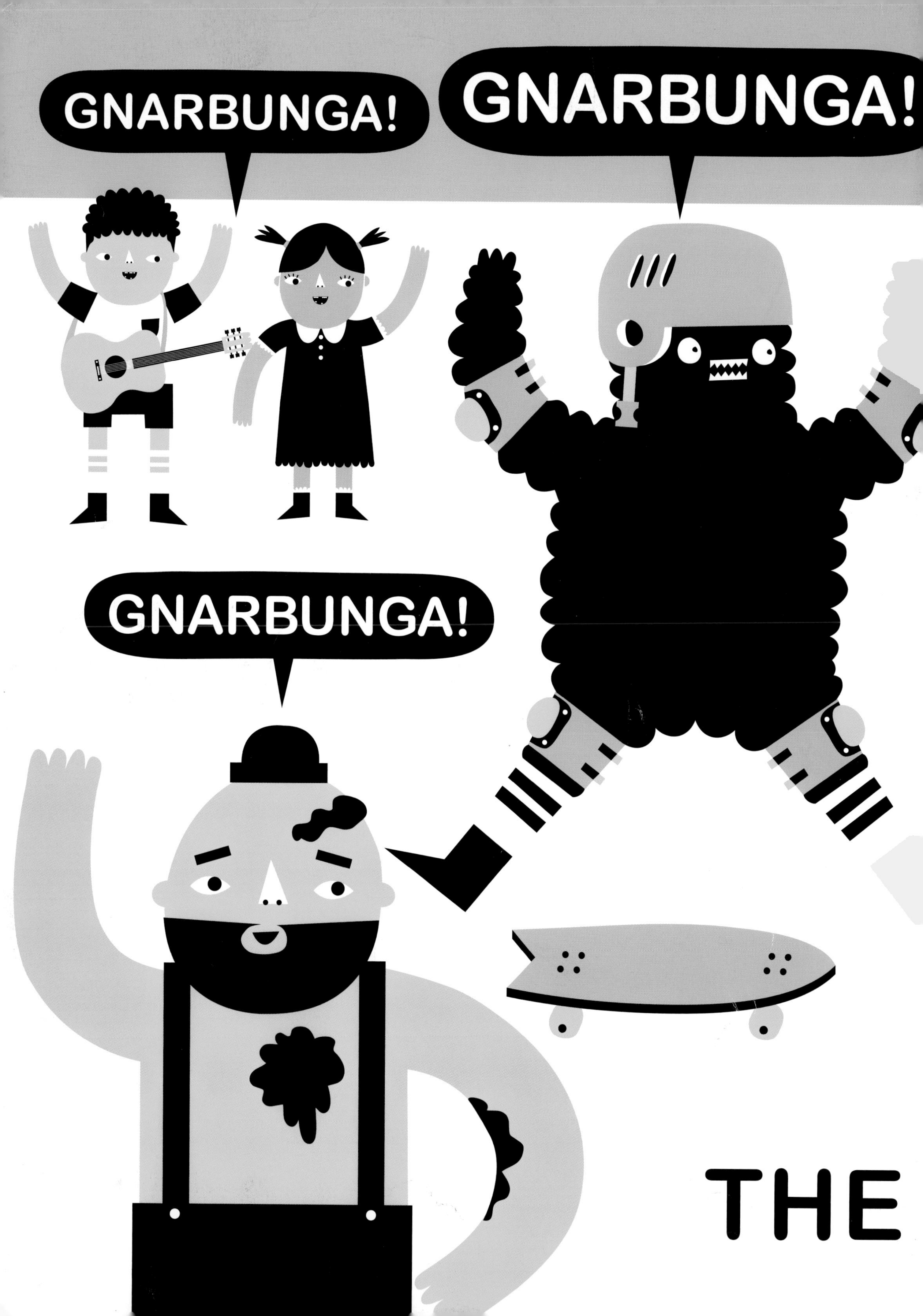
GNARBUNGA!
GNARBUNGA!
GNARBUNGA!
THE

Gnarbunga could even do inverts,
which made everyone shout ...

Gnarbunga learned the best tricks.

He could
kick-flip
over a
cat ...

and do a
boneless
over an
ice cream!

Gnarbunga loved skateboarding.

He said sorry to the people
who didn't like getting icky,
sticky and sludgy.

Gnarbunga got padded
up and was ready to go.

Gnarbunga also had to choose

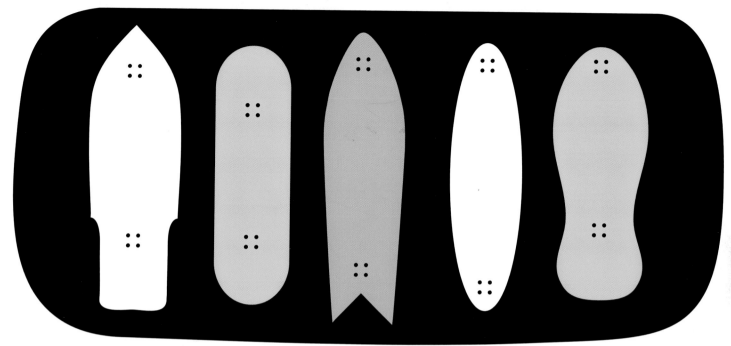

a deck,

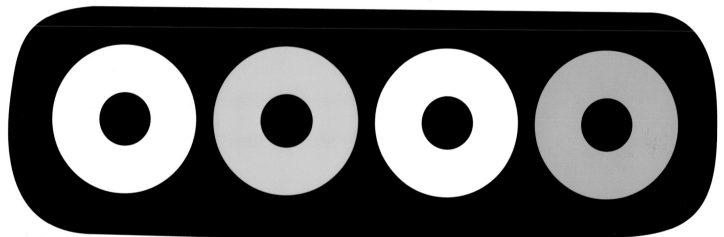

some wheels,

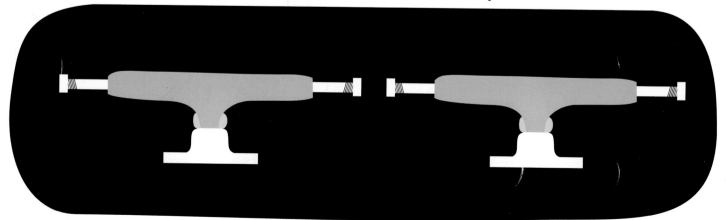

and some trucks!

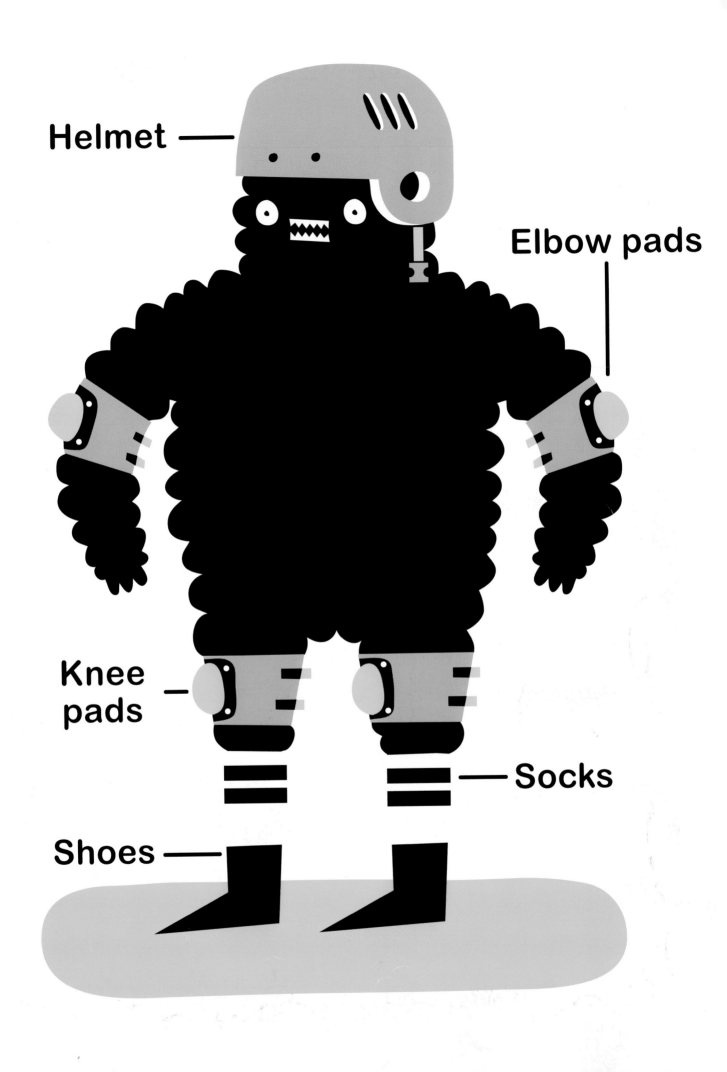

Helmet

Elbow pads

Knee pads

Socks

Shoes

Gnarbunga had to choose

a helmet,

elbow
and
knee
pads,

shoes
and
socks.

help getting started ...

Gnarbunga needed some

So Gnarbunga found something to do and this excited him very much.

Gnarbunga needed some ideas.

But some people
got **very** annoyed!

Some people didn't mind.
They were a little icky,
sticky and sludgy already.

Some people were
not so happy to get icky,
sticky sludge on them.

And they loved it!

Gnarbunga's icky, sticky sludge got all over the children.

Gnarbunga was made
from icky, sticky sludge!

One day Gnarbunga appeared from a mucky, messy hole in the ground.

Written and illustrated by
Matthew Bromley

Boxer Books

For Evgenia Barinova
M.B.

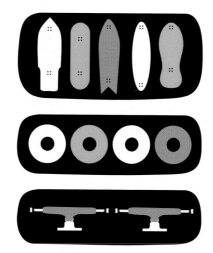

First published in Great Britain in 2012 by Boxer Books Limited.
First published in the United States of America and Canada in 2012 by Boxer Books Limited.
www.boxerbooks.com

Text and illustrations copyright © 2012 Matthew Bromley

The right of Matthew Bromley to be identified as the author and illustrator
of this work has been asserted by him in accordance with
the Copyright, Designs and Patents Act, 1988.

The illustrations were prepared digitally by the author.
The text is set in Adobe Garamond Regular.

ISBN 978-1-907967-14-6

1 3 5 7 9 10 8 6 4 2

Printed in China

All of our papers are sourced from managed forests and renewable resources.